THE EARTH MADE NEW

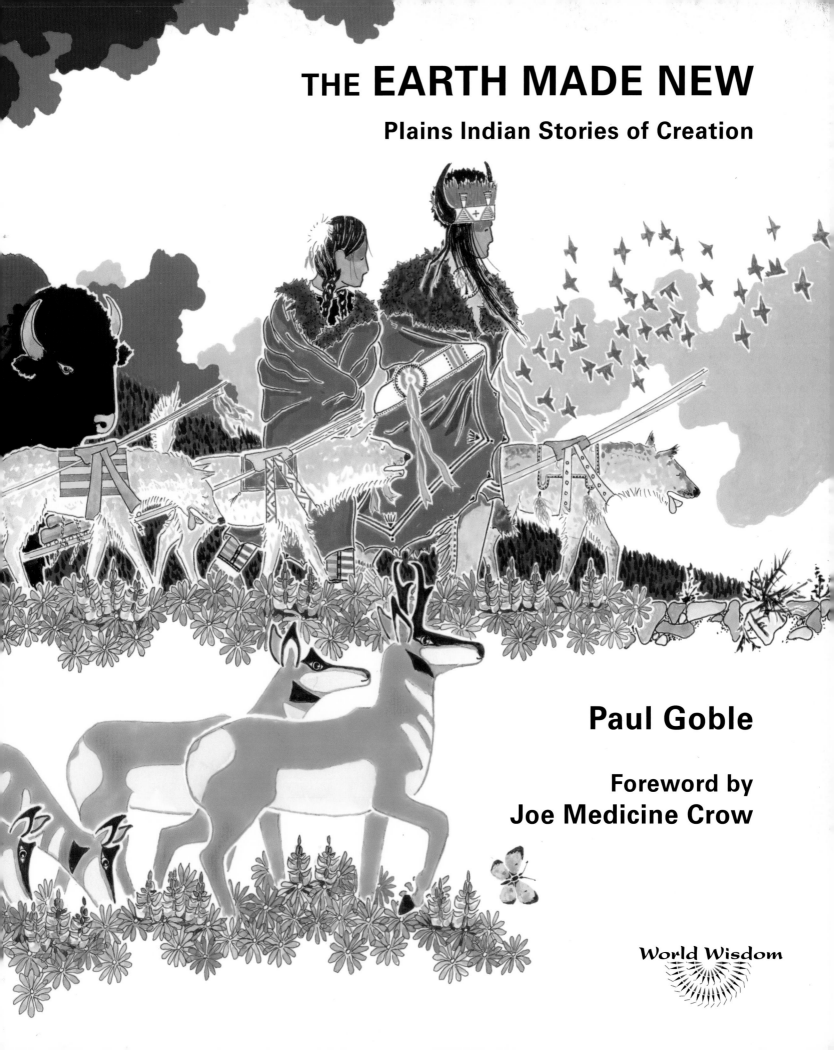

THE **EARTH MADE NEW**

Plains Indian Stories of Creation

Paul Goble

**Foreword by
Joe Medicine Crow**

World Wisdom

Library of Congress Cataloging-in-Publication Goble, Paul. The earth made new : Plains Indian stories of creation / Paul Goble ; foreword by Joe Medicine Crow. p. cm. Includes bibliographical references. ISBN 978-1-933316-67-3 (casebound : alk. paper) 1. Indians of North America--Great Plains--Folklore--Juvenile literature. 2. Creation--Folklore--Juvenile literature. 3. Folklore--Great Plains--Juvenile literature. I. Title. E78.G73G59 2009 398.2089'97078--dc22 2008052910

Printed on acid-free paper in China. For more information address: World Wisdom, Inc. P.O. Box 2682, Bloomington, Indiana 47402-2682. www.worldwisdom.com

References

These are listed with their original publication details, but most are available in recent editions: Joseph Epes Brown, **The Spiritual Legacy of the American Indian**, Crossroad Publishing Company, New York, 1982 (ch. 6); **The Sacred Pipe—Black Elk's Account of the Seven Rites of the Oglala Sioux**, University of Oklahoma Press, Norman, 1953 (9); **Animals of the Soul—Sacred Animals of the Oglala Sioux**, Element Inc., Rockport, 1992; Ella Elizabeth Clark, **Indian Legends from the Northern Rockies**, University of Oklahoma Press, Norman, 1966 (220ff. & 235ff.); W. P. Clark, **The Indian Sign Language**, L. R. Hamersly & Co., Philadelphia, 1885 (42ff.); Natalie Curtis, **The Indians' Book**, Harper & Bros., New York, 1907; James O. Dorsey, **A Study of Siouan Indian Cults**, 11th Annual Report of the Bureau of American Ethnology, Smithsonian Institution, Washington, D.C., 1894; George Amos Dorsey and Alfred L. Kroeber, **Traditions of the Arapaho**, Field Museum of Natural History, Anthropological Series, Vol. V, Chicago, 1903 (1ff.); Richard Erdoes, **The Sound of Flutes and Other Indian Legends**, Pantheon Books, New York, 1976 (126); George Bird Grinnell, **By Cheyenne Campfires**, Yale University Press, New Haven, 1926 (242); **Blackfoot Lodge Tales—The Story of a Prairie People**, Charles Scribner's Sons, New York, 1892 (272); **Some Early Cheyenne Tales**, Journal of American Folk-lore, Vol. XX, No. LXXVIII, 1907 (170); **The Cheyenne Indians—Their History and Ways of Life**, Yale University Press, New Haven, 1923 (90, 91, 337ff.); Alice Marriott and Carol K. Rachlin, **American Indian Mythology**, Thomas Y. Crowell Company, New York, 1968 (21); **Plains Indian Mythology**, Thomas Y. Crowell Company, New York, 1975 (26); James Mooney, **The Ghost-Dance Religion, and the Sioux Outbreak of 1890**, Fourteenth Annual Report of the Bureau of American Ethnology, Part 2, Washington, D.C., 1896 (207); John G. Neihardt, **Black Elk Speaks—Being the Life Story of a Holy Man of the Oglala Sioux**, William Morrow and Co., New York, 1932; Marco Pallis, **The Way and the Mountain**, Peter Owen, London, 1960 (ch. 2); Peter J. Powell, **"Beauty for New Life,"** in **The Native American Heritage, A Survey of North American Indian Art**, University of Nebraska Press, Lincoln, 1977 (44); Lewis Spence, **Myths of the North American Indians**, G. G. Harrap, London, 1914 (107ff.); Stith Thompson, **Tales of the North American Indians**, Indiana University Press, Bloomington, 1929 (Notes 29, 30, 31, 57); Clark Wissler and D. C. Duvall, **Mythology of the Blackfoot Indians**, Anthropological Papers of the American Museum of Natural History, New York, 1909 (7, 8, & 19).

Foreword

Paul Goble has done a good job of presenting the Plains Indian story of creation. There are different variations of this story told among the many tribes; even the Crow people have different variations of the legend about creation. Most of the Crow stories identify Old Man Coyote as the name of the Earth Maker. It is said that long, long ago there was no land—everything was water. Old Man Coyote said, "Let us make land" and sent a duck down into the depths to look for mud. When the duck came up he was unconscious—almost dead—but there was a little bit of mud in his beak. The Earth Maker took this mud and with his medicine power he fashioned it into land. When he finished the world was beautiful, but there was no one to enjoy it. So he sent the duck back down into the depths once again. After the duck returned to the surface the Earth Maker took the mud and made the first man and woman. The storytellers can go on with their account for hours when they add the many details and variations.

In my youth, the storytellers who educated the young children were immediate family members—the grandfathers and grandmothers were our teachers. I remember that my grandfather, whose name was Yellowtail, was my main teacher. I followed him around wherever he went. When he went to go take a sweat bath, I would follow him. While the rocks were heating he told stories like this one. I was fortunate as a boy because so many storytellers were ready to educate the young. Now the television is on all the time and the children no longer follow the elders—they don't take the time to listen to their grandparents. In today's world it is difficult to learn about the olden-day stories, so books that preserve this wisdom have great value.

It is important that our young ones read books about traditional life and values, not just the Indians but all traditional peoples. Paul Goble has created many good books about our Indian ways. He creates good illustrations that accurately present our traditional costumes and crafts. He does careful research to be certain that his stories are authentic and he speaks with the elders to know what they think. The good result is there for all to see.

Joe Medicine Crow
Lodge Grass, Montana

The animals want to communicate with us, but the Great Spirit does not intend they shall do so directly; we must do the greater part in securing an understanding.

Brave Buffalo, Lakota.

Life for the Indian is one of harmony with nature and the things which surround him. The Indian tried to fit in with nature and to understand, not to conquer or rule. Life was a glorious thing, for great contentment comes with the feeling of friendship and kinship with the living things about you.

Standing Bear, Lakota.

Introduction

For Indian peoples, Creation is going on all the time. There were worlds before this one, and there will be others in the future. There is a sense of humor in the stories, like Crow who makes such an annoyingly loud *caw-cawing* that even the Creator has to take notice. Isn't Crow still just the same? There is a sense of experimentation, trial and error, of Earth Maker, the Creator, needing the help of already created beings. These stories, which come from the peoples who lived on the Great Plains, tell that the Creator even left some of his work to his helper, the Trickster, variously known as *Iktomi* (Lakota), *Wihio* (Cheyenne), *Napi* Old Man (Blackfoot). This accounts for the "mistakes" in Creation, like bothersome flies, pesky mosquitoes, ticks.

In ancient times stories of Creation were sometimes told over a ritual four-day period, and included stories about the beginnings of many things: how people were given tipis and fire, the gift of bows and arrows, and the knowledge of how to hunt and make clothes. There were stories which told of people's relationship with the stars, stories about how familiar hills were formed, how birds and animals came to look as they do, the gift of horses, even the coming of white people. These and many others were told prior to important ceremonies which involved all the people, such as the annual Sun Dance and other ceremonies seeking renewal and continuance of Mother Earth's generosity.

Missionaries of every Christian denomination were among the first people to make contact with Indian peoples. They ridiculed the old beliefs with the result that stories, first recorded in the late 1800s, show the influence of the Book of Genesis. This I have tried to filter out. Over the generations, these and other destructive influences of white culture have left only fragments of the traditional stories, but these fragments are as close as we can get to the creation myths told during "Buffalo Days."

I have taken ideas from recorded stories and woven them into the Algonquin "Earth Diver" Creation myth, in which the water birds and animals, which were left behind when the old world was flooded, dive for mud so that the Creator can make dry land again. The elements are mostly Cheyenne, together with others found in Blackfoot and Arapaho stories. I have added Lakota ideas about the end of this world in order to bring the story into our own times, to continue the everlasting cycle of Creation.

When working to retell a Native American story I have always tried to find the earliest recorded versions, because I believe it is necessary to be reminded where the story was in the memory of the people who lived in nomadic times. The oldest records are found mostly in obscure museum and society publications, dating from around 1890 to 1920. It was the period when the last of the "buffalo eaters," those who had lived the old life as adults, were getting old. They saw that their children and grandchildren were growing up in the white world, knowing little about the old nomadic buffalo hunting life which they had lived. Just at that period the new sciences of anthropology and ethnology arose; scientists from museums and other institutions came to the reservations eager to record everything the old people would tell them. It was a meeting of minds: young scientists eager to record, and the elders who wanted what they knew to be preserved for future generations. All manner of aspects of the old life were recorded during this period, including the myths, their sacred stories.

These scientists did not always understand the inner meanings of what they recorded, but they were careful record keepers, and without their work an enormous amount of the culture would have slipped from the collective memory.

I am aware that if the old-time Indian people could come back to life and read what I have written, they would find them very different from what they would tell. By turning to the oldest versions, I feel I get as close as possible to the spirit of the story, which I use as the starting point, but from then on a whole host of changes must take place, from oral to picture book, changes that I am not even aware of. Another influence which must inevitably shape the writing is always the question: can I illustrate it? Inevitably every artist and illustrator is constrained by the limits of what he is able to draw, and this also influences the storytelling.

In addition to seeking out the earliest recorded versions, I like to read more recent renderings where available, and better still to hear Indian people tell me the story in their own words. Sometimes the story is no longer remembered, or it has changed greatly. This I understand because in the main there was a break of generations in the oral storytelling tradition, from around 1900 until about 1965, when the rebirth of Native American cultures began. Those were the melting-pot generations; generations when people of every ethnicity were made to speak English, and to be and act "American."

I have not illustrated Earth Maker as a person because there is no precedent for this in Native American painting. Earth Maker, the Great Spirit, God, is seen in all of his Creation. I have always wanted to name the birds correctly because I think it is only polite. I hope everyone who loves birds will recognize them in my paintings, as those who migrate to the Great Plains in summer, or who live there year long. Water being such an important aspect of these Creation stories, and because water has so many moods and changes, I have tried to paint it in several ways.

When I first talked about doing this book, I was encouraged by my lifelong teacher, Marco Pallis, who said I would have to write it as a "spiritual essay." This I have tried to do, because I always find the writing more difficult than the illustrations. If the language seems to lack descriptive words and phrases, it is nevertheless in keeping with Native American oral tradition: the storyteller picks his words carefully, speaking slowly; often with incremental repetitions, he keeps to the story narrative, while leaving much to the listener's imagination. For the same reason dolls were traditionally made without any features so children could use their own imagination. When writing I try to "hear" the way Edgar Red Cloud used to tell me stories when I was young. He was a well-known Lakota storyteller, tall, handsome, softly spoken, and still of the old oral tradition, for he also spoke with his hands and facial expressions.

All of these things, dear readers and listeners, you must try to see and hear with inward eyes and ears.

Mitakuye oyasin—all my relatives—we are all related.

Paul Goble, Black Hills

LONG AGO THERE WAS ANOTHER WORLD, like our own, but at one time the mountains crumbled, the earth cracked open, and water gushed out, covering everything. Nothing of the old world could be seen above the water: not the tops of the mighty cotton-wood trees, not even the hilltops. It was a time of rain and dark clouds, of dread and calamity.

The only living things were the fishes in the depths and the ducks and animals who lived in the water. The air was filled with the clamor of their wailings. Everyone huddled together swimming hither and thither, crying out in the voice each knew: "Earth Maker!* Earth Maker! We want to live! Give us back the land so we can have a place to make our nests and lay our eggs!"

* Earth Maker is another name for the Creator, the Great Spirit, or God.

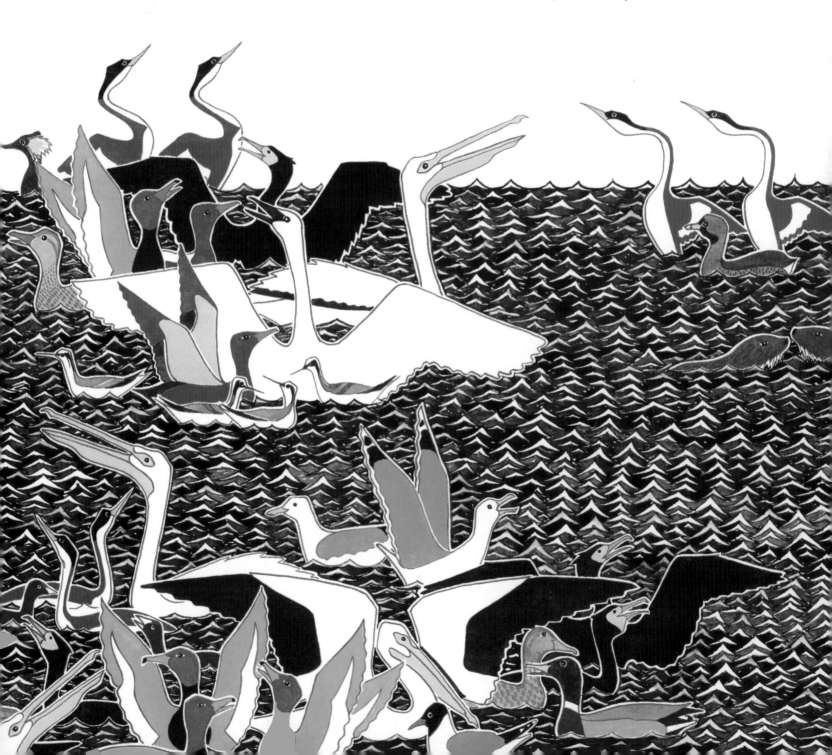

All alone, Crow was flying far and wide over the water. Louder still above the voices of all the other birds, he was calling out indignantly: "*Caw - caw - caw! Caw - caw - caw!* Earth Maker, listen to me! I am tired. Give me some land so I can come down and rest, or I will die. *Caw - caw - caw!* Earth Maker, do you hear me?"

"I hear you," Earth Maker told him. "I will help you," and at his words Crow and everyone took heart. "One of you must help me. I need mud to make land. Who will dive down and bring me some?"

"I will!" Mallard Duck called out. He stretched his neck down into the water, but he could not even see the bottom.*

Earth Maker, the Creator, asked again: "Who will bring me some mud?"

Beaver smacked her broad tail on the water. "I will bring you some mud." She dived, and after her Grebe** dived too, but neither of them could reach the bottom.

* Today Mallards are still searching.

* * Grebe has red eyes as a result.

Earth Maker asked a fourth time: "Is there anyone who can bring me mud?"

"I will try," said the little black Coot, and she dived out of sight. When she did not reappear, everyone thought she had been swept away. Suddenly Earth Maker reached down into the water and brought out the almost lifeless Coot. She was too tired to speak, but there was mud on her beak!*

* Coots proudly wear dried mud on their beaks as a mark of honor.

Earth Maker scraped the mud from the little Coot's beak. "One of you must carry this mud," he said, and everyone wanted to carry it. He looked lovingly at them, and he chose Turtle. "Grandmother Turtle, your back is strong, and you are careful. You will carry this mud. You will always be my joy! Your clothes will be glorious, and all life will come from inside you."*

Earth Maker, the Creator, worked the wet mud in his fingers until it was dry. He sprinkled it on Turtle's shell, and with his power the mud grew and grew until it completely covered Grandmother Turtle and became the earth on which we walk.**

"Come down and rest," he told Crow. "Now all of you can make your nests," and immediately the birds and animals left the water, giving thanks to Earth Maker.

* Turtles walk slowly, remembering Grandmother Turtle who carries the world on her back. When she moves there are earthquakes.
* * North America is called "Turtle Island."

With the power of his imagination, Earth Maker piled up the mountains and smoothed the plains, letting in just enough water to fill the rivers and lakes and prairie ponds. He splashed paints on the ground, red here, yellow and white there.

The mountains he covered with rocks, pine trees, and snow, the plains with grasses and flowers. To everything he gave its own scent, and he composed the music of falling rain and wind in the pine trees.

He made roots and berries grow in their rightful places, turnips, buffalo berries, chokecherries, rosehips, and plums. He made each different: some sweet, some sour, so he did not get tired of any of them.

He scattered cedar trees on the hillsides, and along the streams he planted boxelder trees, willows, and great cottonwood trees so he could enjoy their shade and the sound of their leaves during the heat of the day.

Earth Maker, the Creator, brought into being mighty Thunderbirds with lightning in the blink of their eyes and wings of clouds to carry life-giving rain.*

He hid giant Underwater Monsters in the rivers. He made them battle with the Thunderbirds in the springtime to swell the rivers, flooding the land and filling the swamps, and then everything with roots could drink.**

 * Thunderbirds are careful with their power. It is the young ones
   who cause damage.
 * * When the Underwater Monsters breathe in, water
   spills over and floods the land.

When Earth Maker had finished these things, he peopled the earth with all kinds of beings. He shook the painted robe which he wore, and flocks of happy birds of every color flew out. They understood him when he spoke. In time he gave each one its rightful place to live, and a voice to sing its song of thanks and praise.

Earth Maker spread his robe on the ground, and as he walked slowly, dragging it by one corner, hosts of animals of every kind ran out from underneath. They all understood him when he spoke, and in time he gave each one its place to live.

At first he put the Antelopes among the mountains, but they ran too fast and fell down among the rocks and hurt themselves. He saw that this was wrong and so he led them to the plains, where they could run fast without danger.

In the beginning he told the Bighorn Sheep to live on the plains, but they liked best to jump among the rocks, and so he took them high into the mountains. They loved the cool air in summer, and that is where Earth Maker told them to live.

While Earth Maker, the Creator, was walking around finishing everything, putting Grasshoppers here, Flies there, and Mosquitoes everywhere, he was thinking to himself: "These plains are immense; I will make four-leggeds who are strong and love the hottest sunshine as much as the coldest wind. They will be black and shaggy. The hills and plains will shake with the thunder of their young bulls fighting."

He spread his robe on the ground. Perhaps he was tired, even lay down and fell asleep, because multitudes and multitudes of Buffaloes came out from underneath the edge of his robe and spread out over the plains, everywhere.

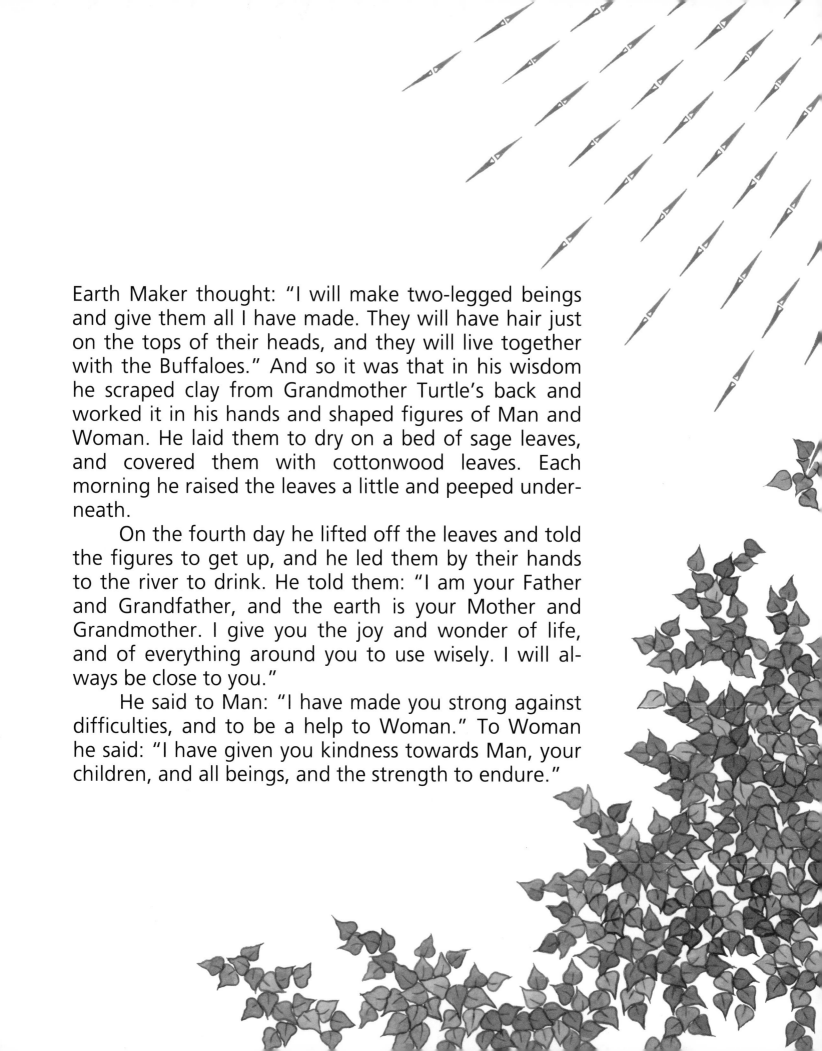

Earth Maker thought: "I will make two-legged beings and give them all I have made. They will have hair just on the tops of their heads, and they will live together with the Buffaloes." And so it was that in his wisdom he scraped clay from Grandmother Turtle's back and worked it in his hands and shaped figures of Man and Woman. He laid them to dry on a bed of sage leaves, and covered them with cottonwood leaves. Each morning he raised the leaves a little and peeped underneath.

On the fourth day he lifted off the leaves and told the figures to get up, and he led them by their hands to the river to drink. He told them: "I am your Father and Grandfather, and the earth is your Mother and Grandmother. I give you the joy and wonder of life, and of everything around you to use wisely. I will always be close to you."

He said to Man: "I have made you strong against difficulties, and to be a help to Woman." To Woman he said: "I have given you kindness towards Man, your children, and all beings, and the strength to endure."

At first People lived in dread of the Buffaloes. Great herds of the huge shaggy black beasts knocked down the tipis and trampled the People to death. Those the Buffaloes did not trample, they chased until they caught, and then *ate* them. . . .* Ya - a - a - a - . . .

Earth Maker, the Creator, heard their prayers for help. He saw how they suffered.

* The long hair on the buffalo's chin is the hair of the people he used to eat.

Earth Maker decided there should be a race of all the birds and animals, around the Black Hills, to decide whether People would eat Buffaloes, or Buffaloes would eat People. The animals sided with the Buffaloes because they have four legs, and the birds with the People because they have two legs. From the multitudes upon multitudes of birds and animals who had gathered, each tribe chose its fastest runner.

Magpie is not a fast flier, but she thinks things out.

Throughout the race she sat on Buffalo's back. When the winning post was in sight, she was not tired, and flew up to win the Great Race for the People.*

"That was a fair race," Earth Maker said. "Now People will eat Buffaloes. But there will always be love between you, and you will live together on these plains until the end of time. Use your power wisely," he warned the People. "Look after all that I have made."

* People honor the birds when they wear their beautiful feathers.

Earth Maker, the Creator, the Great Spirit, loved People so much that he wanted them to talk to him always. It happened this way:

One day when two hunters were looking for the Buffalo, Earth Maker showed them a young woman, very beautiful, dressed in white, carrying a bundle. One of the hunters said she was a holy woman, but the other had bad thoughts, and as she approached, they were suddenly hidden in a mist. When it lifted the foolish one was just a skeleton. The woman told the other hunter: "Don't be afraid. I have a gift for your people. Tell your leader, Standing Hollow Horn, to erect a large tipi, and for all to gather. I will come with the sunrise."

Everyone waited, excited. The mysterious woman appeared as the sun rose, singing while she walked, her breath like a cloud about her in the cold morning air.

She gave her bundle to the leader, and spoke so all could hear: "My brothers and sisters, the Great Spirit has told my Buffalo People to give you this. It is a pipe. You will see your prayers rise up in the smoke, and you will know he always hears you. The pipe will also join families and nations in peace and love, and from today your People and my Buffalo People are one family."

She then left the circle of tipis, and as the People watched, suddenly she was a white Buffalo calf.

Her name is *Pte San Win*, White Buffalo Calf Woman.

Earth Maker wondered how else he could help People. "They have to walk a long way looking for the Buffalo herds. It is hard for the children and old people. I will give them a four-legged who will carry Men and Women on his back. People will feel proud to ride him! I will make him like the sky: gentle and sometimes fierce. He will have lightning in his legs and thunder in his hooves; his mane and tail will be like clouds around him, his eyes bright stars. When People hunt the Buffaloes he will carry them like the wind right among the herds."

And so Earth Maker, the Creator, gave People herds of magnificent Horses of every color.

Earth Maker spoke to the People: "I have promised to always stay close to you. Whenever you need my help on your path through life, talk to me. Sing! I am listening. See your prayers rise up to me in the smoke of your sacred pipes. Look for me on the hilltops and in the mountains. Hear me in the Wind and Water, Crow and Coyote. I will come to you in your dreams and give you the wisdom of the Elk or Eagle, Rock or Thunder. Think about all these, and they will teach you everything you want to know.

"Remember that only the Earth remains forever. Try hard always! Let all beings be happy!"

At the last Earth Maker piled up high mountains to hold back the waters from again flooding the land and engulfing Grandmother Turtle.

He told Bull Buffalo, with his strong curved horns and powerful shoulders, to push against the mountains. Bull Buffalo is strong and he will live for a long time, but not forever! He grows older; every year he loses one hair, and in each of the Four Ages* a leg breaks.** When Bull Buffalo dies the mountains will break apart and the waters will flood in once again, and then . . .

    * The Rock, Bow, Fire, and Pipe Ages.
  ** The wise men have told us that Bull Buffalo is now weak and tired; he stands on only one leg, and he is almost without hair.

. . . Earth Maker will make another world.